W9-BRR-568

C.1

Old Mother Bear

by Victoria Miles
illustrated by Molly Bang

chronicle books·san francisco

AUTHOR'S NOTE

A number of exceptional people, wise in the ways of grizzlies, contributed to *Old Mother Bear.* Special thanks to biologists Erica Mallam, Bruce McLellan, and Wayne McCrory and to veterinarian Darin Collins for providing valuable observations about bears to this story. And for Sandy Watson, Earl Grollman, Ann Featherstone, Andrea Spooner, David Reuther, Elizabeth Harding, and Molly Bang, I am truly grateful.

Text © 2007 by Victoria Miles.
Illustrations © 2007 by Molly Bang.
All rights reserved.

The illustrations in this book were rendered in oils and chalk on Bristol board.
Manufactured in China.

Library of Congress Cataloging-in-Publication Data
Miles, Victoria, 1966-
Old Mother bear / by Victoria Miles ; illustrated by Molly Bang.
p. cm.
Summary: A twenty-four-year-old grizzly bear gives birth to her last litter of cubs, then spends three years
teaching them what they need to know to survive in their southern British Columbia home before
they go off on their own. Includes facts about grizzlies and the Khutzeymateen Grizzly Bear Sanctuary.
ISBN-13: 978-0-8118-5033-9
ISBN-10: 0-8118-5033-1
1. Grizzly bear—Juvenile fiction. 2. Khutzeymateen Grizzly Bear Sanctuary (B.C.)—Juvenile fiction. [1. Grizzly bear—Fiction.
2. Bears—Fiction. 3. Parental behavior in animals—Fiction. 4. Khutzeymateen Grizzly Bear Sanctuary (B.C.)—Fiction.
5. British Columbia—Fiction.] I. Bang, Molly, ill. II. Title.
PZ10.3.M5785Old 2007
[Fic]—dc22
2006011651

Distributed in Canada by Raincoast Books
9050 Shaughnessy Street, Vancouver, British Columbia V6P 6E5

10 9 8 7 6 5 4 3 2 1

Chronicle Books LLC
680 Second Street, San Francisco, California 94107

www.chroniclekids.com

For every bear that ever there was
and especially for "Blanche" and "Aggie" —V. M.

To the Great Bear Foundation,
and to Glacier National Park and all its staff —M. B.

THE OLD SHE-BEAR had been there for three days already, called by the cold to ready her den for winter. Hauling out great mounds of earth and rock, she dug a tunnel down into the half-frozen mountainside.

The grizzly dug until the sky could no longer see the tiny tuck of her tail. Then she began to widen the base of the tunnel. The den was snug, with just enough room to twist and roll, the roof held fast by a tangle of tree roots, the floor blanketed with bear grass and heather.

She had been born in a den like this one, twenty-four summers before. Since the grizzly was three years old, she had made her own dens, always in the high ground, usually on the dark side of a mountain. Sometimes she tunneled into a steep, forested hillside; in other years she squeezed into a cave.

After nine days the den was complete. The tired bear curled up and tucked her nose into her warm belly. Overnight her drowse deepened, her heartbeat and breathing slowed, and her body cooled a little. Snow fell heavy on the mountain. Within a week, the only sign that life slept below was a thin ribbon of gray mist that threaded the dark sky every time the old grizzly exhaled.

Two months went by. When her three cubs were born, Old Mother stirred for the first time since denning. Three pairs of eyes sealed shut could not see their mother. Three pairs of ears tucked down against their heads could not hear her slow, steady breathing. Using their tiny, curved claws, the cubs clung to her fur and on weak, shaking legs, crawled onto her warmest place. There, against her belly, the infant cubs discovered their mother's rich milk.

Days passed. The cubs—two females and one male—
began to crawl. They journeyed over the sleeping giant
and sometimes crossed over the hump on her neck to
nibble on her ears.

Every day, the cubs nursed, napped, grew stronger,
and squabbled. The male sometimes scratched and
bullied his sisters away from their mother's teats.
He fed more often, and quickly grew the largest.

When the old bear finally woke, spring light glowed through
the snow-covered entrance to her den. Her claws, worn
down by months of digging, had grown back to their full
length. She pushed through the wet snow and led the cubs
out above ground.

The cubs were clumsy and unaccustomed to distances.
Halfway down the slope, the old she-bear stopped and scooped
out a groove in the snow where the family could rest. As
she lay back, the cubs clambered over her belly. While they
nursed, their sleepy mother heard their chuckling purrs for
the first time.

The next morning Old Mother lifted her muzzle to learn of a deer, dead many months, down in the valley. When she found it, half-hidden by snow, the carcass was still partly frozen. Old Mother's teeth ached as she bit and tore the meat loose to eat.

For days, the family explored the south-facing slopes where the sun gave spring an early start and the snow had slid away. Old Mother found a few bear berries that had ripened the previous autumn. In the forest, she stripped great hunks of bark from the trees and gnawed at the soft sugary layers underneath. Mostly though, she lived that spring on the first green shoots, leaves, and plant stems.

Wherever their mother went the cubs watched and followed. They padded along ancient grizzly paths where Old Mother had taken all the cubs she'd raised. Sometimes the paths led to scratching posts, where, leaning against a tree, Old Mother rubbed her back. When she parted from the crusty bark, it wore her scent, a little urine, and tufts of her fur.

Spring melted into the early days of summer. The ground thawed and loosened its hold on the mountain. The grizzly could now turn over sods of earth in great chunks to collect the starchy glacier lily corms, bulbs, tubers, and roots that bulged out of the soil.

She rolled over boulders with one paw and stuck her snout into each hole to smell where ground squirrels slept in their underground mazes. Curious, the cubs did the same at every one of their mother's digs. Wherever the smell was promising, she dug furiously to reach her prey. Very few ground squirrels escaped her heavy, stomping paws and the cubs bolted after those that did.

By midsummer, valleys and hillsides were bursting with berries. The cubs watched their mother run her rubbery lips along the length of twig after twig to strip them clean.

A male grizzly, twice Old Mother's size and half her age, came one day to her favorite berry slope. Old Mother knew him, and was afraid for her cubs. As he approached, Old Mother lowered herself to all fours and stepped backward, keeping her young behind her.

The intruder snorted, snapped his teeth, and sprang in the direction of the terrified cubs. Old Mother turned with a "Whuff!" and rushed the cubs ahead of her. But the big male was not content. He charged, and the mountain trembled under the pounding weight of the running bears.

Near the summit, the gap between Old Mother and the big male closed. She turned—sharply—to face him.

Desperate, she drew up tall and roared.

The big male lost his step and stumbled on a boulder. It was just
enough to break the chase, and with one last threatening lunge
he turned back to the berry bushes. Anxious and alert, Old
Mother herded the cubs farther and farther away from the sight
and scent of the big male. It was late afternoon before
she stopped, exhausted and hungry.

In the forest, she tore open the rotting wood of fallen trees for the ants and larvae inside. At his first sight of the squirming insects, the male cub shoved between his sisters to get a lick. He won only a taste before a beetle flew up his muzzle and sent him snorting off the log.

The cubs nursed, napped, and wrestled with each other. Old Mother never played with this litter. She was too tired, and a slow, steady ache accompanied her everywhere. But she tolerated them chewing on her ears, only cuffing the big one away if he bit too hard.

By autumn the bears were almost heavy enough for winter.
With each passing day, as the sky grew darker and colder,
there was less food to find. Old Mother raided squirrel caches
for nuts and ate what berries she found. And the cubs were
strong enough now to dig up roots alongside their mother.

At last the family departed for the high ground. Old Mother
found a cave for them to den in and lined the hard floor
with boughs of fir. Every need but sleep left the bears; all that
remained was to curl up close together.

For two more years, Old Mother led her family over mountains and valleys to the furthest reaches of her range. In their third summer, her young left her. The big male went beyond where his mother roamed and out to the edge of the wild. The two sisters found territories in separate shadows of their mother's range. Both would mate and rear cubs. And every summer, when the huckleberries were ripe, both would trace the tracks of their mother up into the alpine meadows.

In the spring of her twenty-seventh year, the old she-bear awoke in a worn body. She had lost many teeth and those that remained were stained, split, and ground down to her gum line. She was nearly deaf, and soon she would be blind in all but the brightest light. When she rested, it was hard for her to rise from her daybed. So she stayed down longer and foraged less.

Memory and scent were all that remained true. She followed the maps in her mind to swampy patches of skunk cabbage and later up to the huckleberry fields. She ate, but did not gain weight. She no longer hunted, not even for ground squirrels. Her claws were hardly worn at all, she'd scarcely dug all summer, and the muscle between her shoulders had lost its fine swell. She neglected her scent marking, and male grizzlies, in search of a mate, left her alone.

The first call of winter fell upon the old bear early one morning. The snow made her raggedy coat shine and sparkle. The sky held its breath as she rose up to sit on her haunches. A strangeness came upon her. She sat there, still and quiet, all morning long. At last an icy wind summoned her up the mountainside, to a den she knew from long ago. She crept up slowly, and crawled inside.

In the night, a crying storm descended upon the slope. But the grizzly knew nothing of it. She was already gone, past drowse and beyond winter. Her memory she left with every cub she had ever reared; her body she released to the mountain.

The roof of the den collapsed the following spring, and forever after the earth in that place was changed. In time, a warm wind carried to the mountain slope seeds of anemone from far away. And there grew, in that rich country, a field of beauty as never was before.

AFTERWORD

Old Mother Bear is not a true story, but her portrait is based on a grizzly bear in the remote Flathead River Valley of southern British Columbia, along the Montana border. Bear mothers come in many kinds, and like humans, their experience grows as they age. "Blanche," or grizzly #385, is remembered as one of the most intelligent and serious of bear mothers observed by Bruce McLellan, the biologist who recorded her existence.

Blessed are the cubs of an aged mother grizzly. For she has much to teach them, drawn from the course of her lifetime, and their chances of survival are better for what they may learn from her.

Rare is the bear who lives to a ripe old age. Old Mother is one of the fortunate few. A grizzly bear's first challenge is to survive to adulthood. If he is orphaned while still in the care of his mother, he will most likely not live long. And even if he does survive the summer, he will not be strong enough to dig his winter den. The risks to a young bear are many: inexperience leads to deadly mistakes; marauding male grizzlies are a possible threat, as are disease and starvation. A bear may also meet an early end through human contact— whether she is caught riffling through garbage, sniffing around campsites, tempted by apple trees or livestock, crossing a road or railway tracks at the wrong time, or as the deliberate target of poachers or licensed trophy hunters.

Lucky is the grizzly bear born in the sanctuary of British Columbia's Khutzeymateen Valley, where food is plentiful and grizzly bears are protected from hunting. However, few grizzlies live their lives within the borders of safety. One female grizzly's steps might cover a range anywhere from 20 to 400 square miles; a male's range can be thousands of square miles. Outside the bounds of the Khutzeymateen, grizzly bears are vulnerable to a shrinking, altered habitat caused by human demands for the forests, fish, and mineral resources.